Praise for *Little Whale*

Little Whale is a classic addition to the canon of Alaska Native literature for young people. Artist, sculptor, engineer, and now writer, Roy A. Peratrovich, Jr. retells a tale he first heard as a child from his grandfather. Young Kéet's struggles to become a man bounce between reality and imagination. The story is an exciting ride through the trials of men and whales and the churning waters of Southeast Alaska, and it never loses sight of what's really important between a father and a son.

ANNIE BOOCHEVER, author of *Bristol Bay Summer*, 2015 Alaska State Middle School Battle of the Books selection, Literary Classics International Children's Book Award

The stories we tell to our children may be the greatest legacy we can leave. This beautifully written story about a Tlingit boy's coming of age in Southeast Alaska will appeal to Alaska Native and non-Native alike. Roy A. Peratrovich, Jr. weaves historical details of a true story into this narrative, which makes it both believable and compelling. Best of all, the reader identifies with Kéet, who longs to make his father proud even though he is the youngest in his family and small for his age. This is a story worth reading and re-reading. You will love it as much as your children and grandchildren will.

ALEXANDRA J. MCCLANAHAN, author of *Na'eda, Our Friends*

This story of 10-year-old Kéet will immerse young readers in the Native world of Southeastern Alaska. Beautifully written and illustrated, *Little Whale* is an important addition to the Tlingit storytelling tradition.

REBECCA JUDD, Librarian, Bainbridge Island, WA

Roy A. Peratrovich, Jr.'s account of his grandfather's adventure provides a rare glimpse into the daily lives of the Tlingit prior to the changes that occurred with the arrival of Westerners. He captures the worldview of the Tlingit and their spiritual relationship to the environment and wildlife. Perhaps most revealing is the portrayal of the warm, but yet sometimes stern, relationship between father and son. Mr. Peratrovich's story reveals the warmth and humanity of the Tlingit who are more often portrayed as warriors.

ROSITA WORL, President, Sealaska Heritage Institute

I am grateful that Roy A. Peratrovich, Jr. wrote this story. The story incorporates a great deal of cultural knowledge about the Tlingit people and their lifestyle during the time the story takes place. It is a time that is close to us in terms of recently inherited living memory, yet the people who shared those stories and culture with us are all gone now. The culture and customs that are depicted in the story almost completely vanished in the 20th century due to the forces of assimilation and discrimination. It was in the late part of the 20th century that the Tlingit People realized the importance of revitalizing their history, language, culture, and lifestyle.

RANDY WANAMAKER, Deix X'awool Hít, Kaagwaantaan Clan (Two Entrance House of the Kaagwaantaan Clan, Sitka, Alaska), former Director of Goldbelt, Inc.

LITTLE WHALE

LITTLE WHALE

A Story of the Last Tlingit War Canoe

written and illustrated
by Roy A. Peratrovich, Jr.

University of Alaska Press Fairbanks

Text © 2016 University of Alaska Press

Published by
University of Alaska Press
P.O. Box 756240
Fairbanks, AK 99775-6240

Cover and interior by University of Alaska Press

Cover image: Tlingit cedar canoe paddle. © Chris Arend/AlaskaStock.com

Interior images by Roy A. Peratrovich, Jr.

Library of Congress Cataloging-in-Publication Data

Names: Peratrovich, Roy A.
Title: Little whale : a story of the last Tlingit war canoe / by Roy A.
    Peratrovich, Jr.
Description: Fairbanks, AK : University of Alaska Press, 2016. | Summary:
    Long ago in southeastern Alaska, Keet, a ten-year-old Tlingit Indian boy,
    stows away for a voyage on his father's canoe and soon finds himself
    caught in the middle of a wild seastorm that carries him far from his home
    village and, after making land, right in the middle of a dangerous dispute
    between two Indian clans.
Identifiers: LCCN 2015049819 | ISBN 9781602232952 (paperback)
Subjects: LCSH: Tlingit Indians--Alaska–Juvenile fiction. | CYAC: Tlingit
    Indians--Fiction. | Indians of North America--Alaska–Fiction. | Canoes
    and canoeing--Fiction. | Whales–Fiction. | Alaska--History–Fiction. |
    BISAC: FICTION / General.
Classification: LCC PZ7.1.P4475 Li 2016 | DDC [Fic]--dc23
LC record available at http://lccn.loc.gov/2015049819

Printed in the United States by Sheridan
April 2016
Print code: 383336

This book is dedicated to my sons Mike and Doug (Doug is the namesake of Kéet) and my daughter betsy (small "b" intentional–that's how she spells it).

I wish to acknowledge my friend Ann Boochever, my wife Toby, and my daughter betsy Peratrovich, who patiently read through all my drafts. This book would not have been finished without their encouragement and support.

I also want to thank my editors at the University of Alaska Press in Fairbanks, James Engelhardt and Krista West for their wonderful support and encouragement.

And a special thanks to Rosita Worl for authenticating my use of the Tlingit language and customs.

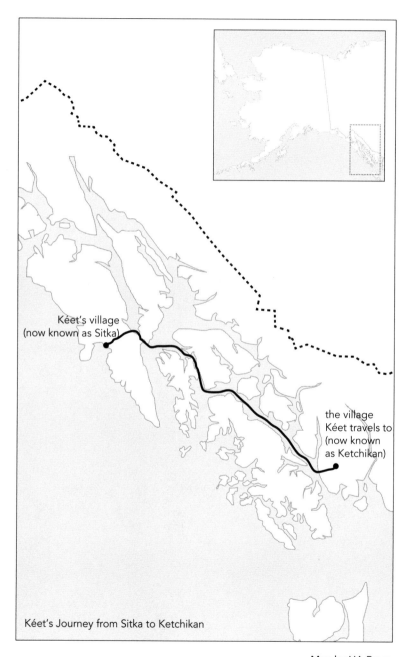

Kéet's village
(now known as Sitka)

the village
Kéet travels to
(now known
as Ketchikan)

Kéet's Journey from Sitka to Ketchikan

Map by UA Press

TABLE OF CONTENTS

WORDS TO KNOW

cháatl   "halibut" in Tlingit

kéet   "killer whale" in Tlingit

gunalchéesh   "thank you" in Tlingit

moiety   The two groups of Tlingit people known as Ravens and Eagles. All Tlingits belong to the moiety of their mother.

saak   A fish called hooligan or smelt today.

shakee.át   "headress" in Tlingit. A hat-like piece of clothing worn by clan leaders.

Tlingit Indians   One of eleven separate cultures of Native people in Southeast Alaska.

yáay   "whale" in Tlingit

INTRODUCTION

Southeast Alaska's Tlingit (pronounced kleen-kit) Indians are one of the four major cultural groups of Alaska Native people.

Tlingit translates loosely to "the People." They survived by hunting, fishing, and gathering the rich resources in Southeast Alaska. They were also great traders, traveling into the interior of Alaska and along the entire northwest coast of North America. The relatively mild climate of Southeast Alaska and the abundant blessings of the land and sea meant that the People did not have to devote all of their time to simply surviving. Thus, many became skilled artists creating a distinctive art form that is known around the world. They created beautiful jewelry and clothing and a variety of elaborately decorated woven, carved, and painted objects, both small and monumental.

The Tlingits believed that spirits exist in every living creature and all forms of nature. Animals, fish, birds, insects, the land and the sea, the sun and the moon, the wind, mountains and rocks, trees and plants . . . in the eyes of the Tlingits, everything has a spirit.

Customs and legends handed down through the generations teach children the importance of taking care of the environment and respecting wildlife, for these are the things that keep the People alive. Tlingit children learn to take only what they need, and they know that anytime something allows itself to be taken, thanks should be given.

Tlingit people are divided into two groups, or "moieties:" Raven or Eagle. Marriage within the same moiety is forbidden, and children assume the same moiety as their mothers. The two moieties are divided into numerous "clans," made up of people who are somewhat related, and the clans are further divided into houses of more closely related people.

The group, clan, and clan house to which a Tlingit belongs is such an important part of his or her identity that it is shared when introductions are made, so that others know who his or her relatives are and where he or she is from.

Along with respecting the environment and wildlife, Tlingits have strict rules of conduct toward other individuals and clans. If someone is offended by another, the clan of the person or clan responsible for the offense needs to atone for it, which sometimes means making a payment. Bad feelings can result if the offense is not properly addressed. In the past, certain offenses could even lead to war.

Clans and houses own property such as hunting, fishing, and berry-picking spots, houses, and ceremonial objects. They even have the exclusive right to use or display family crests and emblems and to perform certain songs and dances. Clans offer protection to members. Clan leaders look out for the clan's property. They also settle disputes and speak on behalf of the clan. Although a highly-regarded clan chief is sometimes considered the village leader, in general, there are not village chiefs who have authority over the entire village.

Years ago, the Tlingits travelled long distances by canoe for trading purposes, marriage, ceremonies, and battle. Their villages were made up of buildings called longhouses, each of which provided shelter to multiple, closely-related families. The houses were built of wood planks–often cedar, but sometimes spruce or hemlock–with wooden screens along the back dividing a separate living space for the clan leader's family. It is here that the clan's valuables were stored. The roofs were supported by four tall house posts, and totem poles graced the outsides of the longhouses. Symbols and crests decorated the house posts, totem poles, wooden screens, and sometimes the walls of the longhouse. The history and legends of the families were depicted with images of animals, birds, insects, and people.

Villages were situated along riverbanks and beaches, with houses facing the water, and mountains or swamps behind. Placing the homes in this manner provided better protection from both bad weather and enemies.

For centuries, the People thrived.

This story is about what might have been the last Tlingit war canoe, if things had gone just a little bit differently . . .

1
THE INVITATION

Long ago, before the white man first set foot on Alaska soil, only Indian tribes lived along the mountainous coastlines and shores of the islands of Southeastern Alaska. The Tlingit Indians are one of those tribes.

This story is about a 10-year-old Tlingit boy who, many years ago, lived in a village now known as Sitka. The boy's name was Kéet, which means Killer Whale in Tlingit. His father was a clan leader and village leader.

Kéet received his name from his great-grandfather, who said he named Kéet after the mighty Killer Whale because he sensed Kéet would one day be a powerful leader himself. Kéet was proud to be named after the Killer Whale, but sometimes wondered if his great-grandfather had made a mistake. Kéet was the youngest in his family, and small for his age. Whenever Kéet's father took his brothers hunting or fishing, Kéet had to stay behind to help his mother gather roots and berries instead.

Kéet wanted to go hunting and fishing with the others more than anything. But no matter how many times he told his father that he wasn't afraid, and that he wanted to go too, his father said Kéet was too young and had to wait a few more years. Kéet felt more and more embarrassed every time he was left behind. Sometimes, he stayed awake worrying that he'd never grow taller and never be able to go. It didn't help that his older brothers enjoyed teasing him by calling him "the little plant hunter." Kéet hated to be laughed at. He longed to make his father proud of him.

Early one morning, Kéet's father gently shook him, waking him from a sound sleep. "Want to go fishing for cháatl with me, Kéet? Come, help me load our canoe."

Kéet jumped out of bed, thrilled at the thought of fishing for halibut with his father. He had always loved the taste of the large, flat fish, but also knew it could be dangerous to fish for them. Some halibut weighed hundreds of pounds. Fish that size could easily hurt a fisherman or damage a canoe. Kéet hoped today would be the day when he could finally prove to his father how brave he was.

Kéet's father had built the morning fire, but everyone else was still asleep. "Be quiet, Kéet, we don't want to wake the others," he warned.

Because his father was clan leader, Kéet's family lived in a separate part of the roomy, cedar-planked longhouse they shared with their close relatives. Kéet was afraid that if he woke his brothers, his father might change his mind and bring them instead, so he quietly tugged on his soft deerskin clothes, slipped on his moccasins, and tiptoed around, gathering the rest of his things before stepping into the large common area.

He was glad to see the other families were still sleeping. They slept on benches under the windows, separated by woven mats hanging from the rafters. The windows were covered with mats as well, except when the weather turned bad—then the men placed huge cedar planks over them.

Kéet knew that the longhouses in other villages did not have windows. The windows had been his father's idea, and Kéet was pretty sure that at first everyone in his village thought his father was crazy. Nobody said anything, though, because that would be impolite. Instead, they simply watched Kéet's father and the other men in his clan cut squares from the wooden sides of their shared home. Their own longhouses were dark inside. The only light came from the shared fire pits, where they gathered to cook as the fire crackled and billowed smoke through the smoke hole in the roof above. Once they saw how much light the windows let in, they asked Kéet's father if they could copy his idea. Kéet's father not only gave his permission, but he and his men helped them cut their windows. Kéet knew his father often had ideas that made life better for the People, and that was one reason his father was considered the village leader.

Kéet hurriedly crept through the low entrance door and stepped outside. It was still dark, but he could see the sun beginning to show above the tall spruce trees behind the village. Kéet thought it was probably going to be a sunny day. He smiled, but stopped when he saw his father looking at him with a curious expression on his face. He didn't want his father to think he was acting like a child. But Kéet's father only smiled back at him. Kéet didn't know that his father was smiling because of how messy Kéet's glossy black hair looked.

The water was calm as Kéet and his father skidded their dugout canoe down to the shoreline. There were many canoes in Kéet's village. Some were made of spruce, and others from cedar. The larger canoes were adorned with carved and painted clan emblems and were used for longer trips involving trading and war. The small canoes, like Kéet's father's canoe, were mainly used for fishing and hunting. The larger canoes held about 20 people and required many paddlers. Kéet's father's canoe held four to six people at most, depending on what supplies they were bringing along. His father had made the canoe by hollowing out a single cedar log. Kéet breathed in the scent deeply. He had always liked the way his father's canoe smelled. It reminded him of the smell of the forest after a heavy rain.

When the canoe was at the water's edge, Kéet and his father loaded it with fishing gear, bait, drinking water, smoked salmon, dried seaweed, and

a handful of fresh blueberries Kéet and his mother had picked earlier in the week. Kéet's father got in the canoe and Kéet pushed it away from shore and climbed quickly into the bow. As they paddled out, Kéet looked back at the village. He saw smoke rising from the homes as the People began the new day.

2
TANGLED IN THE NET

Kéet and his father paddled far from shore to a place where his father knew the halibut liked to feed along the ocean floor at the base of a drop-off. His father handed Kéet the special hook he had made to catch the monstrous bottom fish. The hook was carved of cedar and had a large barb made of sharpened bone. It was designed so that if a halibut was hooked, it flipped the fish upside down. That way, the fish might drown while being pulled up to the boat. There was no chance of a drowned halibut thrashing around and damaging the canoe.

Kéet's father showed him how to attach old salmon heads to the barbed hook. The baited hook was tethered to a rock using a short piece of spruce-root twine. Kéet listened as his father told him how a separate, longer line attached to the hook allowed it to be dropped into the water, while the rock attached to the short line helped it sink to the ocean bottom. The long line could be tugged to make the rock gently bounce along the ocean floor. The baited hook floated freely above the rock in the ocean current, where the halibut could easily see it.

Next, Kéet's father reminded him that they would only be successful catching a halibut if the right words were spoken during the fishing ritual. He showed Kéet the image of a salmon that he'd carved

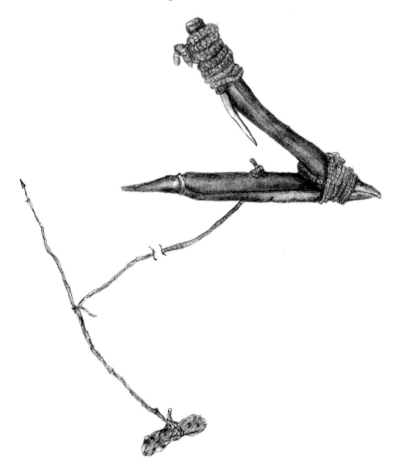

into the hook and that represented the spirit of the salmon. He told Kéet that when the halibut hook was lowered into the water, the Tlingit fisherman would speak to the halibut saying: Wei dei yei jindagút (the spirit of the halibut hook is coming down to you). Akát x'wán yee shíx (come to me; run to me).

They finally dropped their baited hooks over the sides of the canoe, taking care to say the right words, and Kéet began to gently jig his line up and down to attract the halibut. Then they waited, and waited, and waited some more. It was a little chilly, but the sun was beginning to climb in the sky. The waters were still and calm, except for little ripples lapping the sides of the canoe. Kéet and his father were all alone. The village was hidden in the morning mist, and all they could see were occasional smoke trails.

Kéet and his father fished all morning without a single bite. Although his father didn't seem to care, or even be surprised, Kéet was disappointed. He didn't admit it, though, because he figured if he complained, his father might never invite him to go fishing again.

Since he'd missed breakfast, Kéet was very hungry when they finally had lunch, and he ate more smoked salmon than he'd ever eaten. He had always been fond of the salty, sweet fish, and especially liked that when he chewed it, it tasted the way campfires smell. But something about eating it while the cool ocean breeze swept over him made it taste even better.

After lunch, the afternoon sun grew warmer and warmer and ocean swells began to roll in. Kéet and his father pulled up their lines to change the bait, then let the hooks sink to the ocean floor again. The canoe rocked slowly in the ocean swells, and Kéet was having a hard time staying awake. His father was already asleep.

Kéet had dozed off, when suddenly he heard a noise that sounded like someone crying. He sat up and looked around, spying something splashing in the distance. He woke his father and they pulled up their fishing lines, then paddled over to get a closer look. Kéet could hardly believe what they saw: a young whale completely tangled in an abandoned fishing net!

Kéet had never seen a net like this one. His father and the other men used large nets made of cedar-bark twine to fish for saak (today usually called hooligan or smelt). The small, oily fish were very valuable, providing grease for cooking and flavoring. The grease could also be burned to provide light, and was used for trading.

Each spring, huge schools of saak returned to the rivers to spawn. Everyone knew when they were coming because of the squawking seagulls that followed the silvery fish upstream. The men set nets out to catch the saak, and the women hung up ropes to hang the fish to dry.

Sometimes the cedar nets were swept away, but if that happened, they quickly decayed in the salt water and turned into a substance the fish could eat.

Kéet wasn't sure what this net entangling the whale was made of, but it was much larger and thicker than the nets used by the People, and it looked like it had been in the ocean for a long time. He had heard his father and some of the other men talking about the odd strangers that had visited some of the far-away villages. According to the stories, they had boats bigger than the biggest canoe. The strangers were unusually pale, and talked gibberish. They didn't respect their hosts, and were careless in their treatment of animals. Kéet guessed this net had come from the pale people, and it made him sad.

3
THE GIFT

As Kéet looked at the whale more closely, he guessed it was about three times the height of his father. The whale was frightened, but the more it twisted and turned, the tighter the nets became. The poor thing looked exhausted. "Father, we must cut him free before he drowns!"

Having a whale next to the canoe would be much riskier than pulling up a large halibut, but Kéet knew he was right. Whales were special, and the People had the utmost respect for them. They simply could not watch this whale give up its life.

Kéet's father nodded briefly at him before carefully moving the canoe alongside the young whale. "This will be very dangerous, Kéet," he warned. "Don't lean too far over, we don't want to swamp the canoe. And be careful not to cut the whale or yourself."

Kéet took a small knife out of the pouch around his neck. It was made of stone and was very sharp. His father had a larger knife made of bone. The whale continued to thrash and make pitiful sounds as they slowly began to cut the nets off. Suddenly, a flap of skin shifted to cover the whale's blowhole and it ducked its head under the water. When it brought its head up again and breathed out, the flap opened and Kéet was drenched by a fine mist. Then the whale began to struggle and cry again.

Quickly wiping the water from his eyes, Kéet leaned out to gently rub the whale's massive side. Its skin was gray like the round, flat rocks on the beach in front of his village. It felt slippery and smooth under Kéet's hand. He could also see large patches of sharp, crusty-white barnacles, and he made sure not to touch those. Kéet looked into the whale's dark eyes and began speaking to it in a quiet but sure voice.

"Little whale, you are much larger than me, but I can see that you are like me as well, and are not yet full grown. I know you are in trouble, but everything is going to be all right. We are going to help you. But you have to help us too. You have to trust us, little whale. You have to stop fighting."

The young whale looked at Kéet for a long moment, but finally stopped flailing about. Kéet and his father continued to cut and loosen the net until the whale was finally freed. The whale slowly circled their canoe before swimming away toward its mother, who kept a watchful eye on her little one from a safe distance throughout its ordeal. When the young whale reached its mother, both whales leaped out of the water and fell back with a huge double splash. Before long they surfaced, looked back towards the canoe, then turned and dove out of sight again. Kéet heard a series of loud, hollow, knocking sounds coming from beneath the water. His father said it was the whales talking; that they must be saying thank you. Kéet had never heard anything like it before and it sounded magical. The knocking grew fainter and fainter, until all Kéet could hear was the sound of the waves against the side of the canoe.

Kéet and his father leaned back in the canoe, worn out but happy. "Kéet, you were very brave, and you have just saved a young yáay's life. The whale is one of your family clans. They symbolize strength, and you showed much strength in your gentle actions with the young whale. This is a good omen for you."

After resting a bit, they returned to their fishing spot and dropped their lines, and before too long, Kéet hooked his first halibut. It was dreadfully heavy. Kéet's arms grew tired and started to ache as he worked to pull it up, but he was happy that his father let him bring it in by himself.

When Kéet finally got the fish to the surface, he couldn't believe how big it was. Halibut have both eyes on the same side of their heads and their mouths open sideways. Kéet always thought that made them look funny. But when he looked at this halibut, he thought it was the most beautiful fish he had ever seen. He was certain that the halibut had decided to give its life to him because he had saved the halibut's brother, the whale. He bowed his head and gave thanks for the halibut's gift, and when he looked up, he saw his father smiling at him again. This time, Kéet smiled back.

The halibut was too big to pull into the boat without sinking it, so they dragged it behind the canoe all the way back to the beach. Kéet's brothers walked down to help land the fish, and when they saw how big it was they each touched Kéet on the shoulder and nodded solemnly at him. Kéet straightened up and stood as tall as he could. He hoped the days of being called "the little plant hunter" were over.

That evening, the Elders sat around the fire telling stories, as they did every night. Kéet wanted to hear what his father would say about their adventures that day, so he hid in the shadows and listened.

His father started out relating how his youngest son helped to save a young whale's life, and then he told everyone how his son caught the large halibut they had feasted on earlier.

Kéet's face grew warm and red even as he smiled into the darkness. He was still smiling when he heard his father tell the men they must prepare for a long canoe trip. His father said they needed to settle a wrong that had been done to one of their clansmen by a man in a Ketchikan village. They would leave for the other village as soon as the waters were calm. They must bring their weapons, although he hoped they would not need them.

Kéet desperately wanted to go. He'd travelled farther from the village today than he'd ever been before, but he knew there was more to see and he was eager to see it. And being on a war canoe would prove to everyone in the village that he was no longer a boy. Kéet knew that his father would think the trip was too dangerous for him. He came up with a plan. He knew it was a gamble but he decided to stow away aboard his father's canoe.

4

THE ADVENTURE BEGINS

The next day, the men filled canoes with weapons and supplies for the long journey ahead. They packed bows and arrows, spears and war clubs, blankets and extra clothing. They also packed hard-dried smoked fish, fresh berries, dried seaweed, smoked and fresh deer meat, and drinking water.

Kéet waited until everyone was asleep that night. Then he crept down the beach and hid in the bow of his father's canoe, under the sealskin tarp that was wrapped around the provisions.

Early the next morning, the waters were calm. All the canoes shoved off with Kéet's father in the lead canoe. No one discovered Kéet, and for most of the day he slept hidden under the tarp. When he awoke, Kéet liked feeling the water as it flowed under the canoe. He listened to the rhythm of the paddles, but soon grew bored and wished he could lift the tarp to see what was happening.

Shortly before nightfall, the men pulled their canoes ashore on a small island. They made camp on the beach above the high tide line. They built a large campfire, roasted fresh deer meat, and enjoyed a wonderful dinner before bedding down for the night.

The rich aroma of roasted deer meat drifted down to the canoe and made Kéet's mouth water as he lay hidden under the tarp. He waited for what seemed like an eternity. Finally, when the sky was pitch black and he was sure everyone was asleep, he crept slowly up the beach to the smoldering campfire, following the irresistible smell of roasted deer meat. Quietly helping himself to leftovers, Kéet thought he'd never tasted anything better. He ate until his belly poked out a bit. He stretched out next to the fire and began to daydream as he looked up at the moon.

"Kéet, what are you doing here? Where did you come from?"

Startled, Kéet turned to see his father's stern face in the dim fire light. "Father! I thought you were sleeping."

Kéet's father paused before answering. "I was just coming back from a long walk, and I saw your shadow by the campfire. I knew the person wasn't big enough to be one of my men and that might mean trouble. I had my knife ready, until I realized it was you." Kéet's father shook his head, "Kéet, I could have hurt you! And you didn't answer me. What are you doing here? How did you get here?"

Kéet eyed his father's knife and realized how close he'd come to being hurt. He knew he'd let his father down. "I overheard you talking about this trip and I really wanted to come with you, but I was afraid you'd say no. I hid aboard your canoe the night before you left. I'm sorry, father, but everyone treats me like a child. I had to come with you so I can prove that I'm not."

Kéet's father looked at Kéet for a long time before answering. "You should have asked permission to go, Kéet. And you should have thought about how your actions affect others. For one thing, your mother must be worried sick. It is too late now, we cannot turn back. Come with me. It is time we had a talk."

As they walked along the moonlit beach Kéet's father said, "How you treat other people is a measure of the man you will become, Kéet. If you want to be respected, it is important to be honest in everything that you say and do. And if you want people to know that you care about them, you have to show them through your actions and words. Your actions were dishonest and self-centered. I'm not sure if your mother's feelings ever crossed your mind."

Kéet looked down, his eyes filling with tears that he didn't want his father to see. Now he felt ashamed of sneaking around. He remembered the mother whale as she watched her baby, and knew his own mother must be just as worried. His heart ached when he thought of his mother's sadness.

Kéet's father looked at the boy briefly before placing an arm around his shoulder. "I know you love your mother, Kéet, and I know you will try to make up for this. I know how badly you want to grow up and how much you dislike being smaller than your friends. One day you will probably be tall like your brothers, but perhaps not. Either way, you must be patient, and you must trust that things will work out exactly as they are supposed to. You are still young, still learning the ways of the world. But as you learn, you must remember that how you respond to challenges shows others who you are.

"You are not alone in this, Kéet. It is a journey we must all take, and each of us faces different challenges. You may have wondered why I limp when I walk. I was born with one leg shorter than the other, and when I was young like you, I felt inferior to others. But I decided to try harder, to work harder than the others. They told me I'd never be able to run, Kéet, but I practiced all the time, first short distances, and gradually longer. In the beginning, the practice hurt, but I kept on and after a time it hurt less. Eventually, I could run far enough and fast enough that I became one of the best hunters in the village.

"We are all facing challenges on this voyage, Kéet. I must lead us to and from our destination safely, and your presence has added a burden to everyone. They must share their food and drink, and also help to protect you. You must redeem yourself. To do this, you must do your best to help out in any way that you can. You will be our lookout, watching for floating objects that might damage our canoes, and you will also help with camp duties, including the cooking, and gathering and splitting firewood.

"I am also thinking about the respect you need to regain from your mother and our family. When we return home, you will gather and split enough firewood to last the family through the entire winter. You will also haul all of the family's drinking water. Now, let us return to camp."

Kéet's father kept his hand on Kéet's shoulder and smiled down at him. Kéet hugged his father and smiled back, promising to do his best.

That night Kéet slept close to the fire, curled beside his father under a warm mountain goat blanket. Before he fell asleep, he thought for a long time about what his father had said to him. He felt bad for what he had done, but even as his eyes grew heavy, he could hardly wait for sunrise.

5

PREPARING TO CROSS

The next morning, Kéet's father stood beside Kéet as he apologized to the other men and told them how he planned to make up for his mistake. Kéet's stomach was flip-flopping about like a freshly-caught fish. Not only was he embarrassed, he was also afraid that some of the men might be angry with him. Kéet was very relieved when instead they started to make jokes. He knew the jokes were to make him feel better, and didn't mind one bit when some of the men began to call him their "little cook."

After Kéet helped to make breakfast, the men repacked the canoes and shoved them off the beach. The skies were clear and the waters calm for the next few days as the men paddled from island to island. Kéet faithfully watched from the bow of his father's lead canoe for floating logs and other objects. His face turned red in the sun, his hair grew stiff from the cold, salty air, and he was tired more often than not. Kéet never complained, though. He knew keeping watch was very important to atone for his mistake. Besides, he enjoyed seeing all of the wildlife and it sometimes made him forget how tired he was.

One day, Kéet saw a large pod of whales breaching far in the distance and wondered if his new friends might be among them. Thinking about the mother whale and her baby reminded him of his own mother again.

Kéet missed his mother. When he returned home, he would tell her about the deer that roamed the beaches in early morning; their hooves clicking and clacking as they searched for seaweed and licked dried saltwater from the rocks.

He would tell her how later in the day dolphins playfully chased the canoes, while sea otters floated in kelp beds feasting on clams clutched to their dark, glistening chests. And he would tell her about the bowlegged, hunchbacked brown bears that prowled the beaches at dusk.

Kéet would tell her about the schools of herring that swam under the canoes, chased by the salmon who wanted to eat them. And how, in turn, the salmon were sometimes chased by his namesake: Kéet, the Killer Whale.

Kéet could imagine his mother laughing as he described watching Raven, the Trickster, sneaking up behind Eagle and stealing his salmon.

Kéet looked forward to telling his mother about everything he was seeing, but first, he would apologize for causing her to worry about him.

One afternoon, just before nightfall, the men beached the canoes on an island that looked out on a wide expanse of open ocean. While some of the others set up camp, Kéet gathered firewood and helped roast a freshly-killed deer for dinner. After they ate, he listened to the men exchange stories around the smoldering fire. Kéet's father teased one

young man for falling overboard as the canoes were being beached, and another for losing his paddle. There was more teasing, and even more laughter. Kéet began to realize that often when someone teases you, it only means that they like you and are simply being playful. The important thing about teasing is that it should not be harmful or mean.

In spite of the fun they were having, everyone bedded down early. Tomorrow, they would paddle across the open water to islands so far away that they couldn't even see them. The waters were calm that evening, but they all knew a storm could blow in at any time. If that happened, there would be no escaping the giant ocean waves until they reached the protection of the islands on the other side. They needed a good night's rest.

6

RETURNING THE FAVOR

In the morning, dark clouds appeared and strong winds pushed large waves far up the beach, almost into the campsite. It was going to be a long, hard crossing. The men wrapped tarps over the supplies in their canoes, just as they did every day, but today they tied the tarps firmly to the boats. They left the bailing buckets out within easy reach. Kéet made sure to bring a bucket when he jumped into the bow of his father's canoe.

They shoved off after breakfast with Kéet's father's canoe in the lead as usual. The waters were choppy close to shore so Kéet could not stand up in the bow. As they travelled farther out, larger rolling waves began pushing the canoes sideways. The tall trees on the island they left behind shrank and shrank as they paddled on, and soon were just a dark line on the horizon. A while later, a heavy fog drifted in and covered them. Kéet could not see the other canoes. There was nothing but water everywhere. It felt like they were all alone in the world and were being swallowed by the huge ocean.

The men continued paddling as the waves grew bigger and bigger. One moment they were riding the crest of a gigantic wave and looking down at its dark churning bottom, next they were plunging into the trough of that wave, while staring up at the huge, white-topped swell of the next one. Suddenly Kéet was slammed down so hard that he cried out in surprise and ended up swallowing a mouthful of saltwater. He felt like he might get sick. He was glad he had a bailing bucket, just in case.

Then it began to rain. At first just a light patter, then hard. Seawater came in over the sides of the canoe while the men bailed and paddled as hard as they could. Kéet was bailing so fast his hands got numb from the cold water. He was afraid he might accidentally drop his bucket. Soon the seawater surged in faster than they could bail it out and it became harder and harder to balance the canoes. Some provisions washed overboard, and what didn't go overboard got soaked. Everyone was wet, cold, and exhausted, but with the strong wind behind them and a following sea, they couldn't go back, only forward. Kéet was afraid they would never reach land.

Suddenly, an enormous bump jarred the canoe. It felt like they were being lifted on another huge wave, only this time, the canoe didn't slide back down. Had they hit a large log that Kéet had not seen? He peered over the side and was astonished to see the broad, gray back of a large whale. Their canoe must have landed atop the whale's back.

Kéet's father yelled to everyone to hang on because the whale could dive at any moment. Its immense tail fin could be very dangerous if it hit them. But the whale kept swimming near the surface with the canoe balanced on its back. When the fog cleared, Kéet could see that the other canoes were also riding atop the backs of whales. A familiar, sharp squeal burst from the water near him, and Kéet turned to see the same young whale that he and his father had rescued. Kéet knew without a doubt that they were being saved by the young whale's pod. His father's canoe was being carried on the mother whale's back. The whales they had seen earlier had followed them and were now helping them.

The men bailed the rest of the seawater out of the canoes and salvaged what supplies they could. Meanwhile, Kéet searched for signs of land. At long last, mountains appeared through the heavy blanket of clouds. "Land ahead!" he cried. The whales had carried the canoes to the safety of a protected inlet, and with a final lift of their huge tails, they launched the canoes toward the beach.

A short time later, they saw the whales surface again in the distance. The whales played and breached over and over, and Kéet could hear the now-familiar knocking sounds carrying over the water. The men had been saved by the whales, and the whales were celebrating! Kéet could hardly wait to get onshore to dry off and hear the others' stories.

7

THE CONFRONTATION

When the men woke the next day, the waters were calm and the dark clouds gone. They soon started on their way again. The next few days were uneventful as they continued on to their destination. Seven days after the storm, Kéet saw smoke trails rising in the distance. His father said the smoke marked the village of Ketchikan.

As the canoes drew closer, Kéet's father told the men to follow his canoe to an island directly across a narrow inlet from Ketchikan. He said he didn't want the villagers to feel threatened by landing all of the canoes at once. He would go alone to meet with the village leader. The men were to wait there until he returned.

Although the purpose of their trip was to settle a wrong that had been done to one of their clansmen, Kéet's father reminded the men that he did not wish to fight. Then he took Kéet aside. "Kéet, I will be back, but while I am gone you must do as the men tell you." Kéet hugged his father and helped him push off in his canoe.

As Kéet's father paddled across the small inlet, Kéet could see the villagers gathering at the top of the beach. Some of them had weapons. The tide was out when the canoe touched the shore. Kéet saw his father step out of the canoe and slowly limp up the long, rocky beach toward the villagers.

Kéet's father carried no weapons. The villagers shouted at him not to come any closer, but he continued to slowly approach them anyway. With no further warning, the villagers began throwing spears at Kéet's father. "No! No! No! He's not armed!" Kéet yelled. He ran toward one of the nearest canoes, but the men grabbed Kéet and told him to wait. It looked like the villagers were purposely missing his father with their spears.

As Kéet's father got closer, the Ketchikan village leader ordered his men to stop attacking. Then he stepped forward to meet the stranger. After talking for a few minutes, the Ketchikan leader nodded to Kéet's father and Kéet's father signaled to his men to let them know he was all right. Then he and the Ketchikan leader disappeared into the village.

A while later, the two men returned to the beach and Kéet's father proudly waved something that looked like a long, thick stick to his men across the inlet. The men cheered loudly as Kéet's father paddled back across the inlet. Then they gathered around to hear what had happened.

"There will be no battle; we have agreed on a settlement. After introducing myself as the Sitka leader, I explained to the Ketchikan leader that we came a long way to right a wrong done to one of our clansmen by one of theirs. I told him I wished to settle the matter–that we were ready to fight, but that if he and I could reach an agreement, there was no need for war.

"The Ketchikan leader invited me to his lodge and someone brought local tea. We drank tea for a short time. Then, after listening to my story, the Ketchikan leader agreed that a wrong had been done and a debt was owed. We agreed that the debt would be settled according to Tlingit custom.

"The Ketchikan leader invited us to a ceremony tonight in our honor. He also gave me a very special gift. It is called a black-powder musket. He said it is extremely powerful and will help us to hunt better than with our arrows or spears. He will show me how to use it before we leave."

Kéet's father passed the musket around so that everyone could admire at it. He let Kéet touch it, too. Kéet took a deep breath, relieved that nothing bad had happened to his father and that there would be no fighting. His father had settled things with words and nobody would get hurt. Kéet could tell that the other men were relieved as well, even if they didn't say so. He was very proud of his father.

8

THE PEACE CEREMONY

Kéet and the rest of the Sitka clan had been traveling and camping for many days. They took care to clean themselves up for the ceremony, bathing in a nearby freshwater stream. Kéet even remembered to comb his hair. After all, ceremonies were only held on special occasions. Kéet had been to ceremonies when someone got married or had children, and he'd also been to others held to honor people who died. He knew ceremonies were for a few other reasons as well, like payment of a debt, but he'd never been to one like this before.

Shortly before paddling to the Ketchikan village, the men donned ceremonial attire. Kéet was glad that the special clothing hadn't been washed overboard— especially his father's Chilkat robe and dance apron. Only highly respected and well-off leaders wore Chilkat robes. Nobody else could afford them. They were woven from mountain goat wool and cedar-bark strips, by members of the Chilkat clans. It could take more than a year to make just one robe. Kéet's father had traded many cedar boxes, spruce-root baskets, rabbit and goatskin blankets, and horn spoons for his robe.

Kéet watched in awe as his father got dressed. As his father pulled his apron on and wrapped his robe around himself, Kéet admired the long fringe and

the bright blue and yellow dyes in the designs. No wonder they were so expensive! Next, Kéet's father put on his shakee.át (headdress). The headdress had a wooden front piece with a frog crest carved on its face. The top was adorned with sea lion whiskers and raven feathers, while snowy white ermine furs framed his father's face and cascaded down his back.

Lastly, Kéet's father painted his face with ceremonial markings. When his father was finally ready, Kéet looked at him proudly and thought how handsome he looked. One day, he hoped to be as handsome and wise as his father.

Kéet didn't have any ceremonial clothes but he changed into a clean set of deerskin clothing that he'd brought along, tugged a headband on, and made sure the pouch holding his knife hung outside of his shirt where it could be seen.

After the other men dressed, some of them painted their faces. Kéet glanced around and saw that several of the men were wearing only breech cloths so that their tattoos would show. Others were dressed in leggings and tunics. Many had put on bracelets or necklaces. Some had on wooden hats and masks shaped and painted to look like animals. Some had on spruce-root hats, and some wore colorful button blankets. Everyone looked magnificent, he thought. Then it was time to go.

Kéet had the most fun he could remember at the ceremony. All of the Ketchikan villagers were there, and they had also dressed in their finest. Kéet made many new, young friends and entertained them with stories about the trip and his adventures with the whales.

The evening began with a lavish banquet, which was good because Kéet was starving. Everyone feasted on fresh deer, goat and moose meat, baked salmon and halibut, herring and salmon eggs, dried seaweed, smoked salmon, seagull eggs, fresh berries, fried bread, soap berries, and—a first for Kéet—chicken eggs. The chickens had been left behind by one of the boats of pale people that had stopped at the Ketchikan village. The pale ones had apparently traded the musket and the live chickens for sea otter pelts. Kéet had never seen chickens before that day, and he laughed out loud watching the scraggly birds jerk and strut about while making strange noises and scratching at the ground. He'd heard the pale ones were odd, so he guessed it was only natural that their birds were odd as well. Kéet imagined telling his mother about the chickens and wondered if she would believe him.

After dinner, there were ceremonial dances, singing, speeches, and storytelling. The ceremony lasted all evening. At the end of the night, Kéet's father gave the Ketchikan leader a beautiful painted ceremonial paddle in return for the village's generosity.

The following morning when the men began to prepare the canoes for the long trip home, they were surprised to discover that the villagers had restocked their provisions, including leftover food from the ceremony and fresh water. Kéet's father thanked the villagers once again for their kindness, and then they all said their goodbyes.

As Kéet pushed his father's canoe into the water, he heard strange noises coming from under the tarp. He carefully lifted one corner to peek underneath

and could hardly believe his eyes when he saw three live chickens tethered together—a gift from his new friends. What a surprise—his mother would have to believe him now! Kéet waved to his friends as he stood proudly in the bow of his father's canoe.

One day soon Kéet hoped to return, but for now he was eager to get home and see his mother and brothers. He smiled when he realized he wouldn't even care if his brothers continued to call him "the little plant hunter." Kéet figured that he was a good plant hunter, and had turned out to be a pretty good cook, and he now knew that his grandfather had been right all along: one day, he'd be a good leader just like his father. He just had to be patient. As the canoes began to move, Kéet wondered if he'd ever see the whales again.

Kéet's father rose in the canoe and shouted his thanks, "Gunalchéesh!" to the men on shore. It had been a very successful journey.

AUTHOR'S NOTES

Little Whale is based on a real-life adventure of my grandfather, the late Andrew Wanamaker, when he was a small boy living in Sitka, Alaska. Andrew was a full-blooded Tlingit, who later in life became a Presbyterian minister in Southeastern Alaska. Kéet was not his name, but it happens to be the name he gave to my youngest son, Doug. I chose to use the name because of Doug's determination and spirited outlook on life, and because its meaning fit my story.

Andrew was only 10 years old when he and his sister were invited to accompany their father on a 200-mile canoe trip from Sitka to a village located where Ketchikan is today. A clan member in the Ketchikan village had done a wrong to a member of my grandfather's tribal clan. According to Tlingit custom, a tribal leader whose clan member was injured must seek payment from the clan that inflicted the injury to settle the wrong. Andrew's father, my great-grandfather, was the tribal leader that led the way to the Ketchikan village. My grandfather never told me the nature of the wrong.

My grandfather and his sister travelled in the bow of their father's canoe where they slept under a covering, just like Kéet in this story. His father's canoe was the lead canoe. All the canoes were armed for battle, just in case.

Due to poor weather and high seas, it took about 10 days for them to reach Ketchikan. When they arrived at Ketchikan, all the canoes pulled ashore on an island facing the village, and from this point, Andrew's father paddled alone and unarmed to the Ketchikan village, where he was shot at. Thankfully, the shots missed.

Had there been a battle, this could have been the last, or one of the last, Tlingit battles. Instead, the issue was settled peacefully with a wonderful ceremony, where Andrew saw his first chicken.

As a young man living in Southeastern Alaska, I have shared experiences similar to my little hero, Kéet. I have enjoyed the beautiful scenery and wildlife in Southeastern Alaska and witnessed many colorful Tlingit ceremonial dances. I have enjoyed all kinds of local "Indian foods," wild berries and wild game, and have done my fair share of hunting and fishing. I have also been caught in some pretty rough and terrifying seas in small boats, although perhaps not quite as bad as Kéet's experience.

The part of this story about the whales didn't really happen on my grandfather's adventure. At least he never said it did . . .

Roy Andrew Peratrovich Jr.
Yéil Hít Lukaax.ádi Clan
(Raven House of the Sockeye Clan)